Ainslee Bunch
Eva Bew

Ainslee Bunch
Eva Bew

Treasury of CHRISTMAS
Stories for Families

COMPILED BY
ROBERT VAN DE WEYER

ILLUSTRATIONS BY
DEBORAH KINDRED

Copyright © 1994 by Hunt & Thorpe
Illustrated © 1994 Deborah Kindred
Published in Nashville, Tennessee, USA,
by Dimensions for Living

ISBN 0-687-07821-0

In Clean Hay, from The Christmas Nightingale by Eric P. Kelly, copyright
1932 the Macmillan Company, New York.

94 95 96 97 98 99 00 01 02 03 – 10 9 8 7 6 5 4 3 2 1

This book is printed on acid-free recycled paper.

Manufactured in Hong Kong

Designed by The Pinpoint Design Company

INTRODUCTION

Long before Charles Dickens wrote "A Christmas Carol", people were telling stories about Christmas. All manner of legends have grown up around the birth of Jesus himself. And even more tales have been woven around the celebration of Christmas. Perhaps we are so familiar with the real events of Christmas, recounted in the Bible, that we need stories to reawaken us to its true meaning. And perhaps, too, we just enjoy gathering round the fire with our loved ones on December evenings, sharing the wonder of Christmas in any way that our imagination allows.

There is a third reason for telling Christmas stories – at least, as far as I am concerned. As a pastor, I find myself preaching each year at about a dozen services over the Christmas period, I cannot for the life of me think of a dozen ways to expound the Christmas message in an ordinary sermon. So instead, I tell stories.

This is a collection of stories told from the pulpit, and re-told at numerous school assemblies. Some I have gleaned from ancient sources, others came from my own head. Pastors like myself, and teachers too, may find them useful. Most of all, I would love them to be read aloud to the family by the fireside on a dark December evening.

CONTENTS

The Fourth Wise Man
6

The Shepherd's Son
11

Baboushka
16

Papa Panov's Visitors
21

The Lost Boat
26

Why The Chimes Rang
30

The Stubborn Tree
34

In Clean Hay
38

Pastor Noodle's Light
44

The Little Fir Tree
48

The Third Lamb
53

The Christmas Juggler
58

THE FOURTH WISE MAN

When the star appeared in the sky on the first Christmas night, four wise men from the East set off on the long journey to Bethlehem. But only three arrived in time to see the baby Jesus. The fourth was too late. Yet he was the kindest, bravest and wisest of them all. His name was Artaban.

Each of the wise men packed precious gifts for Jesus. The other three had gold, frankincense and myrrh. Artaban took three beautiful jewels; a ruby, a sapphire and a diamond.

They set off at midnight and travelled without stopping. But as the sun rose, they saw a man lying beside the road. Artaban got off his camel and knelt beside the man, but the others hurried on.

The man told Artaban that robbers had stabbed him and taken all his money. Artaban lifted the man onto his camel, and took him to an inn. He gave the innkeeper the ruby and asked him to care for the man. Then he climbed onto his

camel and rode off, travelling as quickly as he could.

The next day, late in the afternoon, Artaban saw a woman sitting by the side of a road, holding a tiny baby. The woman was dressed in rags, and both she and her baby were shivering.

Artaban stopped and got off his camel. The woman told him that her husband had died just after their baby was born, and since she had no money, the landlord had thrown her out of her cottage.

Artaban lifted the woman and her baby on to his camel, and led them to a nearby town. It was now almost dark, so they spent that night at an inn. The following day, Artaban looked for a place where the woman and her baby could live. At last he found a white cottage for sale. With a heavy heart, he gave the owner the sapphire. Now he only had the diamond to give to Jesus. But when he took the woman and her baby to the cottage, her joy was so great, that Artaban felt happy, said goodbye, and continued on his journey.

At last he arrived in Bethlehem. But to his horror, he found soldiers striding from house to house, with blood on their swords. The people told him that King Herod had given

7

orders that every boy under the age of two should be killed.

Artaban rushed to find the richest merchant in town. He gave him his diamond in exchange for gold coins, and then ran around Bethlehem paying each soldier a gold coin to stop killing baby boys. He told families to hurry from the city before King Herod found out. When every family had left, Artaban himself rode off as fast as he could – knowing that if King Herod ever found him, he would be executed.

Thirty years later, when Artaban was a very old man, he heard stories of a man called Jesus who had been born in Bethlehem, and was now attracting great crowds with his teaching and healing. Artaban knew that this must have been the Jesus whom he had tried to visit all those years ago. He decided to make the journey once again and offer Jesus a jewel, as he had tried to do before. He sold all his possessions, and bought a huge white pearl.

Once again, he came to Bethlehem. But he was told that Jesus was now in Jerusalem. Just outside Jerusalem, he saw a crowd lining the road. To his horror, they told him that Jesus was about to be crucified.

Then he saw Jesus, followed by three men, all carrying heavy crosses. He held up his pearl, eager to give it to Jesus. But one of the men saw it and cried out that he was innocent of the crimes for which he was being punished. He said that if he died, his wife and children would have no one to support them. He begged Artaban to use that pearl to buy his freedom.

Artaban looked at Jesus, and Jesus smiled and nodded. Artaban offered the pearl to the officer in charge of the prisoners. And the innocent man was set free.

So Artaban never gave any jewels to Jesus. But when Jesus smiled and nodded to him, he knew that in truth all his jewels had been given to Jesus — because whenever we serve those in need, we serve Jesus. And as he watched the crucifixion of Jesus, he learned something else. Just as he had paid for that prisoner's freedom with his pearl, so Jesus paid for the freedom of every person in the world by his death.

REJOICE AND BE MERRY

1

Rejoice and be merry in songs and in mirth:
   O praise our Redeemer, all mortals on earth!
For this is the birthday of Jesus our King
   Who brought us salvation – his praises we'll sing.

2

A heavenly vision appeared in the sky;
   Vast numbers of angels the shepherds did spy
Proclaiming the birthday of Jesus our King
   Who brought us salvation – his praises we'll sing.

3

Likewise a bright star in the sky did appear,
   Which led the wise men from the east to draw near;
They found the Messiah, sweet Jesus our King
   who brought us salvation – his praises we'll sing.

4

And when they were come, they their treasures unfold,
   And unto him offer myrrh, incense and gold:
So blessed for ever be Jesus our King
   Who brought us salvation – his praises we'll sing.

DORSET CHURCH-GALLERY BOOK

THE SHEPHERD'S SON

Very early on the first Christmas morning, a shepherd burst into his cottage.

"Wake up," he cried to his wife and son. "A most amazing thing happened last night. I was looking after our sheep, when suddenly a bright light shone across the sky. Then a voice started speaking."

"What did it say?" asked his son, sitting up in bed.

"It told us to go into Bethlehem to see a baby that had just been born – a baby who would save the world." He described how he and other shepherds had rushed into Bethlehem and seen the baby Jesus lying in a manger, with his mother Mary beside him.

"I'd like to take a present to the baby Jesus, " said the shepherd's son.

"That would be very nice, Benji," said his mother, "but we've no money to spare."

After breakfast, Benji walked out into the fields, wracking his brain to think of a present. Suddenly he spotted fluffy pieces of lamb's wool caught on a hedge – and he had an idea.

All day, Benji walked round the fields, picking pieces of wool from the hedges and brambles. In the evening, he sewed a cloth bag and pushed the wool inside to make a soft pillow.

That night as he lay in bed, Benji's heart thumped with excitement. He woke at the crack of dawn, leaped out of bed and hastily swallowed his breakfast. Then he set off for Bethlehem. He knew he must hurry if he was to get there and back before nightfall.

After a while, he met a girl sitting on a log. She was clutching a tiny, shivering bird.

"What's wrong with that baby bird?" asked Benji.

"The poor thing has lost its mother," the girl replied, "and it's dying of cold."

Benji looked at his pillow full of wool, and then at the tiny bird. The bird was cheeping, as if begging for help, but each cheep was softer than the last. Slowly, Benji opened the pillow and took out enough wool to wrap round the bird. As the bird grew warmer, its cheep became stronger.

Benji continued on his way. A mile further on, he met an old man with a camel. On the camel's back was a heavy pack. One corner of the pack was rubbing against the camel's side, making a nasty sore.

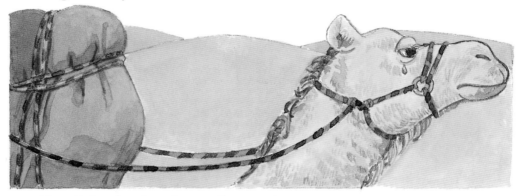

Benji looked at his pillow of wool, and then at the camel. It was panting and snorting, as if asking for help.

Benji found himself reaching into the pillow, and taking out a wad of wool. He placed it carefully under the side of the pack where it had been rubbing the camel's skin.

"Thank you, little friend," the old man said.

Benji had spent so long with the bird and the camel that by the time he came near to Bethlehem, the sun was setting. Ahead of him he saw a man leading a donkey; and on the donkey was a young woman with a cloak drawn around her. As they approached, Benji could hear them speaking.

"You must be very uncomfortable sitting on the bare back of a donkey," the man was saying.

"God will look after us," the young woman replied. But her voice sounded so weary that Benji longed to help her.

Tears welled up in his eyes. "If I give her my pillow," he thought, "I'll have nothing to give to baby Jesus."

But he knew what he must do. Benji went up to the man and woman, and offered them his pillow.

"That is most generous!" exclaimed the man.

The young woman smiled at Benji, and climbed down from the donkey. Then Benji saw a tiny baby in her arms under her cloak.

"Please," said the young woman, "could you take a piece of wool from the pillow to put on my shoulder – for the baby Jesus to rest his head?"

Benji could hardly believe his ears. He stood staring at the woman and the baby.

"We shall always be grateful to you," said the man. "Now we must hurry. We're going to Egypt to escape from those trying to kill us."

Benji stood in the middle of the road, and watched the man, the young woman, the donkey and Jesus disappear over the hill. Then he let out a great yelp of delight, and danced up to Bethlehem.

That evening, a kindly innkeeper let Benji sleep in his stable.

"Do you know," said the innkeeper, "last night a baby was born in this stable, and he slept in that manger over there."

Benji went over to the manger and climbed into it. There was just room to curl up snugly. And even though a cold wind was blowing, the hay still felt warm, as if Jesus had only just been taken out.

ALL MY HEART THIS NIGHT REJOICES

1

All my heart this night rejoices
    As I hear, far and near,
Sweetest angel-voices:
    "Christ is born!" their choirs are singing,
Till the air everywhere
    Now with joy is ringing.

2

Hark! a voice from yonder manger,
    Soft and sweet, doth entreat:
"Flee from woe and danger;
    People come; from all doth grieve you
You are freed; all you need
    I will surely give you."

3

Come then, let us hasten yonder;
    Here let all, great and small,
Kneel in awe and wonder;
    Love him who with love is yearning;
Hail the star that from far
    Bright with hoe is burning.

4

Thee, O Lord, with love I'll cherish,
    Live to thee, and with thee
Dying, shall not perish,
    But shall dwell with thee for ever
Far on high in the joy
    That can alter never.

Paulus Gerhardt (1607-76)
translated by Catherine Winkworth (1827-78)

BABOUSHKA

From a traditional Russian story

Baboushka lived all alone in a little wooden cottage near the road that linked Palestine with the great cities of Asia. She welcomed travellers into her cottage, giving them stew cooked in a huge copper saucepan that stood above an open fire. People enjoyed coming because the stew was so delicious, and because Baboushka herself was so cheerful. So they were happy to pay her well. She kept the money she received in a large wooden box under her bed, and over the years she had collected quite a large sum.

Most of the travellers who came to her cottage were ordinary merchants, with spices and silks piled high on their camels. But one evening, three tall men walked through the door, dressed in magnificent robes, with crowns on their heads. Baboushka was so astonished at the sight of these men that she could not speak.

"May we have supper here?" one of the men asked. Baboushka, still unable to speak, beckoned them to the table, and served three large bowls of stew.

"This is the finest stew I've ever tasted," said another of the men. By this time, Baboushka had regained her voice. She asked the three men who they were, and where they were going.

They explained that they were three kings from countries far to the east.

"We are travelling towards Palestine, in search of a baby who has been born to be a king – the king of all the kings. And we have gifts for his wonderful baby – gold, frankincense and myrrh." Baboushka's eyes lit up at the thought of the baby born to be king. She had always loved babies, and longed to see this baby for herself.

"Where is the baby?" she asked.

"We do not know," they replied, " but there is a star guiding us."

Baboushka looked out of her window. Sure enough, there was a star above her cottage.

When they finished supper, the three kings asked if there was anywhere near by where they could stay for the night.

"I am afraid there are no inns for many miles," Baboushka replied, "but you are welcome to stay in my bedroom."

The following morning, Baboushka gave the kings a large breakfast. Then they said goodbye, climbed onto their camels, and rode off. Baboushka stood in the road, watching them disappear into the distance, with the star hovering above them. When they were no more than tiny specks on the horizon, Baboushka heaved a huge sigh, and went back into the cottage to continue her work.

But she could not concentrate on what she was doing. She kept thinking of that special baby to whom the kings were taking such precious gifts. She began to think of the gifts she would like to give. "I'm sure," she said to herself, "that he would like some nice toys. After all, even royal children like playing." Then she heaved another sigh. "I have so much cooking and cleaning to do that I can't possibly set off on a journey in search of this baby."

But suddenly, hardly knowing what she was doing, she leapt to her feet and rushed into her bedroom. She pulled the wooden box out from under the bed, took out the money, and ran out of the house. She hurried to the town and

bought all the best toys she could find. She put them in a large sack, and set off along the road after the three kings.

There was no star to guide her. And her two old legs could not possibly go as fast as the kings' camels. At every town and at every crossroads, she asked people if they had seen three kings passing that way. But no one had seen any sign of them. And most people thought she must be mad to ask such a question.

After a month, she realised she was completely lost. She did not know where to find the baby. Nor did she know the way home. Her heart began to sink, and tears welled up in her eyes. But then a strange peace came over her. She knew that, even if she never saw him, she could still make the baby happy – she would give her toys to every sick and unhappy child she could find.

So, for the rest of her life, Baboushka trudged from village to village, from town to town, seeking out sick and unhappy children. To each one, she gave one of the toys in her sack. And, strange to say, the sack never got emptier. There were always enough toys for everyone.

IN THE BLEAK MID-WINTER

1
In the bleak mid-winter
    Frosty wind made moan,
Earth stood hard as iron,
    Water like a stone;
Snow had fallen, snow on snow,
    Snow on snow,
In the bleak mid-winter
    Long ago.

2
Our God, heaven cannot hold him,
    Nor earth sustain;
Heaven and earth shall flee away
    When he comes to reign:
In the bleak mid-winter
    A stable place sufficed
The Lord God almighty,
    Jesus Christ.

3
What can I give him,
    Poor as I am?
If I were a shepherd
    I would bring a lamb;
If I were a wise man
    I would do my part;
Yet what I can give him –
    Give my heart.

Christina Georgina Rossetti (1830-94)

PAPA PANOV'S VISITORS

From a story by Leo Tolstoy

As dusk fell on Christmas eve, old Papa closed the shutters of his shoemaker's shop. He felt very sad. Children's laughter in the street reminded him of his own children, who had grown up and moved far away, and mothers' voices calling their children reminded him of his own wife, who had died earlier that year.

He sat on his rocking chair by the fire, and opened his big old family Bible. He read again the Christmas story of how Mary and Joseph, tired from their journey, could find no room at the inn.

"Oh dear," he said. "If only they had come here! I could have given them my bed." His sadness lifted at the thought of welcoming the holy family to his home.

He read of the three wise men bringing their gifts. Papa Panov felt sad again. "I have no gift I could give Jesus," he said.

Then suddenly his face brightened. He hurried into his workshop. From the highest shelf, he took down a small, dusty box. Inside were two tiny leather shoes. He had made them years ago for his own baby son. But he had taken so long that, by the time he had finished, his son's feet were too big for them.

"These are the finest shoes I've ever made," he said. "I could give these to the baby Jesus."

He closed the box and went back to his chair. He opened the Bible again, but by now he was so sleepy that his eyes closed before he could read another word. As he slept, he had a strange dream. It seemed as if Jesus was in his room.

"You have been wishing that you could see me," Jesus said in a gentle voice. "Look for me tomorrow, and I will visit you."

Papa Panov awoke the next morning to the sound of church bells. "Bless my soul!" he blurted out. "I've spent all night in my chair!" Then he remembered that it was Christmas day. As he cooked his porridge, Papa Panov thought about his dream. He felt sure that it would come true. After breakfast, he went out to look for Jesus.

The street was deserted, shrouded in a layer of snow. Around the corner came the village road sweeper, clearing a path for people to walk to church later that morning.

"Happy Christmas!" cried out Papa Panov. "Come in and have a hot cup of coffee." The road sweeper, whose hands and feet were numb with cold, was delighted. He sat on Papa Panov's rocking chair in front of the fire, and drank a mug of coffee. Then he returned to his work, whistling a carol.

Papa Panov put some cabbage on the stove and went out again into the street. After a time, a girl approached, walking very slowly. As she drew nearer, Papa Panov could see that she was carrying a baby underneath her shawl. "Please come into my house," he said, and beckoned her to sit down on the rocking chair. He gave her a large bowl of cabbage soup, and warmed some milk for the baby. The baby's feet were bare and blue with cold. "He needs shoes," Papa Panov said.

"I can't afford shoes," the girl replied. "My husband has died and I'm on my way to the next village, to work as a servant."

Papa Panov remembered the tiny shoes he had made for his own son. He went into the workshop, and returned with the dusty box. Carefully, he put the shoes on the baby's feet. They fitted perfectly.

The girl now rose from the rocking chair, wrapping her baby under her shawl, and walked to the door. "You have been so kind to us," she said. "May God bless you, and make all your Christmas wishes come true,"

As the girl and her baby disappeared down the snowy street, Papa Panov began to think that his Christmas wish would not come true. It was now almost dark and there was no sign of Jesus. He sat down on his rocking chair. "It would have been wonderful if Jesus had visited me," he said. "But if he had come, I would have had nothing to give him." He sighed, thinking of those beautiful little shoes.

He put his Bible on his knees. It fell open at the Gospel of Matthew. As Papa Panov read the words, he could hear in his head the same voice that had spoken to him in the dream. "I was hungry and you gave me food," the voice said. "I was thirsty and you gave me a drink. I was a stranger and you welcomed me."

Papa Panov looked up. "So you did come and visit me after all," he said. And his wrinkled face broke into a broad smile.

O LITTLE TOWN

O little town of Bethlehem,
    How still we see thee lie!
Above thy deep and dreamless sleep
    The silent stars go by:
Yet in thy dark streets shineth
    The everlasting Light;
The hopes and fears of all the years
    Are met in thee tonight.

2
For Christ is born of Mary
    And, gathered all above,
While mortals sleep, the angels keep
    Their watch of wondering love.
O morning stars, together
    Proclaim the holy birth,
And praises sing to God the King
    And peace to all the earth.

3
How silently, how silently
    The wondrous gift is given!
So God imparts to human hearts
    The blessings of his heaven:
No ear may hear his coming,
    But in this world of sin
Where meek souls will receive him, still
    The dear Christ enters in.

4
O holy Child of Bethlehem,
    Descend to us, we pray;
Cast out our sin, and enter in,
    Be born in us today!
We hear the Christmas angels
    The great glad tidings tell:
O come to us, abide with us,
    Our Lord Emmanuel!

Phillips Brooks (1835-93)

25

THE LOST BOAT

Jeremy lived by the sea. Whenever he could, he liked to go down to the beach to watch the fishermen push their boats into the waves, and later on, haul their boats back up to the beach, their nets full of fish. Jeremy dreamed that one day he would have a boat of his own.

His father knew that Jeremy wanted a boat. But since Jeremy was too young to go out to sea in a proper boat, he decided to make a large model boat which Jeremy could play with. Every evening in October, November and December, Jeremy's father went to his workshop to build the model boat. Jeremy knew that his father was making something very special, but he was not allowed in the workshop to see what it was. At last, on Christmas Eve, Jeremy's father finished the boat. He wrapped it carefully in paper and put it under the tree.

On Christmas Day, when Jeremy unwrapped his father's present, he could not believe his eyes. The model was exactly like the fishermen's boats down on the beach, only much smaller. It even had two sails which Jeremy could hoist and lower, just as the fishermen hoisted their sails as they went out to sea, and lowered them again when they returned to shore.

Jeremy was so excited that he insisted on going down to the beach straight away, even though the weather was bitterly cold. He and his father put on their wading boots and warm coats, and carried the boat down to the sea. They waded a short distance through the rough waves, and then Jeremy hoisted the sails and launched the boat into the water.

For about half an hour, Jeremy and his father watched the beautiful boat bobbing about on the waves. The wind was blowing towards the shore, and the tide was coming in, so that even if Jeremy pushed his boat out to sea, it soon came back again. When the tide was about to turn, Jeremy's father said they should go back home.

"Let the boat have one more trip!" cried Jeremy, and pushed it as far out to sea as he could manage. But at that moment, the wind changed direction, catching the sails of the boat and blowing it away from the shore. Jeremy was horrified, and began to wade after his boat. But his father grabbed his arm and pulled him back. Together they stood and watched the beautiful boat sail out to the open sea. It grew smaller and smaller, until finally it was such a tiny speck in the distance that they lost sight of it. Jeremy cried out loud. And tears trickled down his father's cheeks, as he remembered all the work in making the boat.

The rest of Christmas Day was miserable. Even the juicy Christmas pudding his mother had made could not bring a smile to Jeremy's lips. And when he went to bed, he cried himself to sleep.

On the following day, Jeremy was still miserable. But on the day after that, his father took Jeremy to the shops along the sea front to see if they could buy a new boat. Jeremy was certain that no boat could be as fine as the boat his father had made. Despite his father's encouragement, he did not want any of the new model boats they saw.

Finally they reached a small, dirty second-hand shop, down a little alley. Jeremy's father went in, but Jeremy stayed outside, convinced that such a place could not have any boat worth possessing. Jeremy's father picked his way through the dusty goods piled high. Then suddenly his eyes lit up. Perched on top of an old wardrobe was his boat, the boat he had built for his son.

"Where did you get that?" he asked the shopkeeper.

"Oh," the shopkeeper replied, "it was washed up on the beach on this morning's tide."

Jeremy's father said no more but gave the shopkeeper the money he wanted for it. Then he rushed out of the shop and handed the boat to Jeremy.

"My...my boat!" spluttered Jeremy.

"Yes, it's yours," said his father. "In fact, it's doubly yours. I made it for you, and now I've bought it for you. So you take care of it properly now."

As they walked home, Jeremy's father felt very happy. He had been a true father. In his small way, he had done for his child what our heavenly Father has done for all his children. Our Father God made the world for us. And when we spoilt what he had given us, he bought it back for us by sending his Son at Christmas. And so the world is doubly ours to love and to care for.

THE OXEN

Christmas Eve, and twelve of the clock.
    "Now they are all on their knees,"
An elder said as we sat in a flock
    By the embers in hearthside ease.

We pictured the meek mild creatures where
    They dwelt in their strawy pen,
Nor did it occur to one of us there
    To doubt they were kneeling then.

So fair a fancy few would weave
    In these years! Yet, I feel,
If someone said on Christmas Eve,
    "Come; see the oxen kneel!

"In the lonely barton by yonder coomb
    Our childhood used to know,"
I should go with him in the gloom,
    Hoping it might be so.

Thomas Hardy (1840–1928)

29

WHY THE CHIMES RANG

From a story by Raymond MacDonald Alden

In a far away country, there was once a wonderful church. It stood on a hill in the midst of a famous city, and every Sunday thousands of people climbed up to its great archway. No church such as this was ever seen before.

At one corner was a tall grey tower with ivy growing over it. Up and up climbed the stones and the ivy, as far as the eye could see. All the people knew that at the top of the tower was a chime of bells. They had hung there ever since the church had been built and were the most beautiful bells in the world. Some said they sounded like angels far up in the sky; others like strange winds singing through the trees. They were Christmas bells, made to be rung on Christmas Day. But, strange to say, for many long years the bells had never been heard.

It was the custom on Christmas Eve for all the people to bring their offerings to the Christ child. It used to be that when the greatest offering had been laid on the altar, through the music of the choir they would hear the Christmas chimes far up in the tower. But now, it was said, people no longer brought offerings great enough to deserve the music of the chimes. Every Christmas Eve, the church was crowded with those who thought that perhaps the wonderful bells might

ring again. But only the roar of the wind could be heard far up in the stone tower.

Now a few miles from the city, there lived a boy named Pedro and his Little Brother. They knew very little about the Christmas chimes, but they had heard of the service on Christmas Eve and often talked about the beautiful celebration. One year they made a secret plan to go to the church on Christmas Eve.

That year, the day before Christmas was bitterly cold, with a few snowflakes flying through the air. Pedro and Little Brother were able to slip quietly away early in the afternoon. Before nightfall, they saw the lights of the city ahead of them.

They were about to enter one of the great city gates when they saw something dark in the snow near their path. It was a poor woman, too ill to go any further.

Pedro knelt down and tried to rouse her. After a moment, he said, "It's no use, Little Brother. You will have to go on alone."

"Alone?" cried Little Brother.

"Yes," said Pedro, sadly. "This poor woman will freeze to death if nobody cares for her. Everybody has gone to the church now. When you come back you can bring someone to help her. I will rub her to keep her from freezing, and perhaps get her to eat the bun in my pocket."

"But I cannot bear to leave you," said Little Brother.

"You can easily find your way to the church," Pedro said. "You must see and hear everything twice, Little Brother –

once for you and once for me. Take this little silver piece and lay it on the altar when no one is looking. Do not forget where you have left me."

As Little Brother hurried off to the city, Pedro winked hard to keep back the tears. It was hard to lose the music and splendour of the Christmas celebration and spend the time in that lonely place in the snow.

The great church was a wonderful place that night. When the organ played and the thousands of people sang, the walls shook.

At the close of service came the presentation of the offerings. Rich men and great men marched proudly up to the altar. Some brought wonderful jewels, some baskets of gold. A famous writer laid down a book that he had been writing for years. And last of all walked the king. He took off his crown, all set with precious stones, as his offering.

"Surely" everyone said, "we shall hear the bells now."

But only the cold wind was heard in the tower.

The procession was over, and the choir began the closing hymn. Suddenly the organist stopped playing as though he had been shot. All the people strained to listen. Softly through the silence came the distant sound of chimes. So sweet were the notes, rising and falling away up there in the sky, that people sat for a moment. Then they all stood up and stared at the altar to see what great gift had awakened the bells.

But all that the nearest saw was Little Brother, who had crept down the aisle and laid Pedro's little piece of silver on the altar.

RING OUT WILD BELLS

Ring out wild bells to the wild sky,
    The flying cloud, the frosty light:
The year is dying in the night;
    Ring out, wild bells, and let him die.

Ring out the old, ring in the new,
    Ring, happy bells, across the snow:
The year is going, let him go;
    Ring out the false, ring in the true.

Ring out old shapes of foul disease,
    Ring out the narrowing lust of gold;
Ring out the thousand wars of old,
    Ring in the thousand years of peace.

Ring in the valiant man and free,
    The larger heart the kindlier hand;
Ring out the darkness of the land,
    Ring in the Christ that is to be.

From IN MEMORIAM
by Alfred, Lord Tennyson (1809–32)

THE STUBBORN TREE

The Protheroe family had a large garden. And in one corner they grew little fir trees. So every Christmas Eve, instead of buying a Christmas tree, Grandad Protheroe used to go out in the garden and pull up one of the trees. He would promptly carry it into the house, and plant it in a bucket of earth. Then the four Protheroe children would decorate it with tinsel and lights.

One Christmas Eve it was snowing very hard. Grandad put on a white scarf, a little red bobble hat, and a thick red coat, and trudged out into the snow. The children sat at the window to watch.

Grandad knew which tree he wanted. He brushed the snow off the branches and began to pull. But it would not come. He pushed it forward and back, hoping to loosen its roots, but still it would not come.

He felt a little silly, knowing that the children were watching him – and probably laughing at him. But he had to trudge back to the house and ask the oldest child, called Mark, to come and help him. Mark was twelve, and Grandad was sure that between them they could pull up the tree. Mark himself felt rather proud, thinking that his strength would make all the difference.

So Mark put on his coat and scarf and trudged through the snow with Grandad. He stood behind Grandad, with his arms round Grandad's stomach, and together they pulled. But the tree would not come.

They pushed it forward and back, but still it would not come.

Now they felt silly. Mark trudged back and fetched Andrew, aged nine. Andrew put his arms around Mark's stomach and pulled.

But the tree would not come.

They pushed it forward and back, but still it would not come.

They felt very stupid. Andrew trudged back and fetched Simon, aged six. Simon put his arms round Andrew's stomach, and the four of them pulled. But the tree would not come. They pushed it forward and back but still it would not come.

They began to think that they would not have a Christmas tree that year. Only little Lucy, aged three, was left in the house and they did not think she would be much use. But Simon trudged back and fetched her.

Lucy felt rather frightened as she put on her coat and scarf. She did not think she could possibly make any difference, and she was worried that her big brothers would blame her.

They formed a line. Grandad was in the front, holding the tree. Then came Mark, holding Grandad. Then Andrew, holding Mark. Then Simon, holding Andrew. And finally little Lucy, holding Simon.

"One, two, three, HEAVE," shouted Grandad. and they pulled with all their strength. Suddenly they could hear the root snap, and the tree lifted out of the ground. As it came, they all fell backwards into the snow, laughing with pleasure.

When they had carried the tree back to the house and taken off their coats, Grandad put his arm round Lucy.

"Well," he began, "I think we have all learned something about Christmas this year. The smallest child makes the greatest difference. And just as little Lucy caused that stubborn tree to move, so the little child Jesus can move the most stubborn hearts."

A CRADLE SONG

Sweet dreams, form a shade
    O'er my lovely infant's head;
Sweet dreams of pleasant streams
    By happy, silent, moony beams.

Sweet sleep, with soft down
    Weave thy brows an infant crown.
Sweet sleep, Angel mild,
    Hover o'er my happy child.

Sweet smiles, in the night
    Hover over my delight;
Sweet smiles, mother's smiles,
    All the livelong night beguiles.

Sleep, sleep, happy child,
    All creation slept and smil'd;
Sleep, sleep, happy sleep,
    While o'er thee thy mother weep.

Sweet babe, in thy face
    Holy image I can trace.
Sweet babe once like thee,
    Thy Maker lay and wept for me,

Wept for me, for thee, for all,
    When He was an infant small.
Thou His image ever see,
    Heavenly face that smiles on thee,

Smiles on thee, on me, on all;
    Who became an infant small.
Infant smiles are His own smiles;
    Heaven and earth to peace beguiles.

William Blake

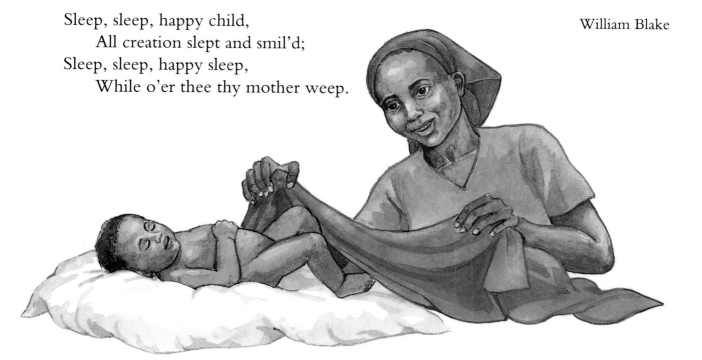

IN CLEAN HAY

From a story by Eric P. Kelly

In a farmhouse a few miles outside the old Polish city of Krakow, a boy is reading the newspaper to his family. "Tomorrow is Christmas Eve," he reads, "and Krakow will have many visitors. This year a famous performer will give his puppet play, the Szopka Krakowska, at the Falcon Hall…"

The boy, whose name is Antek, puts down his paper. "Our puppet show is all ready."

His father says, "Don't stay out too late."

"No, we won't," Antek says. "We'll give our show several times, and then come home."

In one corner of the room stands a small, wooden, two-towered church. At its base, large doors stand open, revealing a stage, and wooden dolls in bright clothes. This is the puppet theatre – a Szopka Krakowska.

Their mother comes in with a huge pot of soup. "Well, tomorrow you will go out with the Szopka," she says.

"Yes. And make lots of money!" This is from Stefan, younger than fifteen-year-old Antek.

"And what will you do with the money?"

A clamour goes up from the four children. The farm is poor and this chance of making a little money means a great deal. Every year they look forward to Christmas when, since the earliest days of the city, boys have given puppet shows in Krakow.

The children start out about one o'clock. As they near the city, the sun is sinking and the lights are coming on. In the market place, they mount the puppet theatre on its legs. A crowd gathers. They have just started when a man orders the play to stop.

"Don't bother us!" shouts Stefan.

"Where is your license?" the man asks.

"License?"

"Yes. You must have a license to give public performances."

"We didn't last year," Antek says.

"You must this year. Move along or I'll report you."

"Come quick!" orders Antek, snatching up the theatre. "We'll have to go home."

Anusia, who is ten, begins to cry. Just then, two men who are busy talking, bump into the children.

"Look out there!" says one. Suddenly he stops and exclaims, "A Szopka, as I live!"

"A Szopka!" the second man says, in amazement.

"Yes, and a good one," says the first man, looking at it quickly. "Here is an answer to our prayers. Do you people operate the Szopka?"

"Yes."

"Do you want an engagement?"

"Yes!"

"Then come with us. We were to have found a famous Szopka tonight. Pan Kowalski and his wife. But there is no Pan Kowalski. We've looked everywhere."

The men stop in front of a building on which there is a figure of a falcon. "In here."

While the children get the show ready, one of the men talks to the audience. Then Christopher plays the trumpet, lights come on in the towers, and Anusia sings an old hymn. Before the people of Krakow, the puppets act out the beautiful Christmas story. It is splendid. Stefan reads the voices, Antek makes the puppets dance as if they are alive, Anusia sings like an angel, and Christopher's violin plays merrily.

When the collection is taken, the bowl is heaped high. It

is the best day's work that any Szopka has ever done. The crowd leaves slowly, and the four, beaming with delight, set off for home.

On the way, they stop at a neighbour's house for a rest. He tells them to come to the stable. "I had no room in the house," he explains. "The hay is warm and there is a stove."

They enter the stable. Then they draw in their breaths and fall on their knees.

There, by the manger, is a young woman and in her arms a little baby.

"It is the Christ child," whispers Stefan. "And there is the place where the Wise Men knelt." He points. Indeed, a dark figure stands up and looks round.

"It is Pan Kowalski, the puppet-show man," says their neighbour. "He was on his way to Krakow. He and his wife stopped here, and while they were here, the baby was born. They have no money. They were to have received much money for their puppet show. I do not know what they will do. The show is only given on Christmas Eve."

"And it was the night that Christ was born..." says Antek. The four children go outside. They look at each other.

"Let me go back," says Stefan. He creeps into the stable, and listens to the quiet breathing of the mother. Then he goes to the manger and drops in all the money from the collection. He falls upon his knees for a moment, and says a prayer.

As he runs back, a most wonderful happiness seizes hold of him. There, upon the Krakow road, Christ is born again in the hearts of four happy children.

CHRISTMAS BELLS

I heard the bells on Christmas Day,
    Their old familiar carols play,
And wild and sweet,
    The words repeat,
Of "Peace on earth, good will to men!"

And thought how, as the day had come,
    The belfries of all Christendom
Had rolled along
    The unbroken song,
Of "Peace on earth, good will to men!"

Till ringing, singing on its way,
    The world revolved from night to day –
A voice, a chime
    A chant sublime,
Of "Peace on earth, good will to men!"

And in despair I bowed my head,
    "There is no place on earth," I said,
"For hate is strong
    And mocks the sound
Of "Peace on earth, good will to men!"

Then peeled the bells more loud and deep:
    "God is not dead, nor doth he sleep!
The wrong shall fail,
    The right prevail,
With peace on earth, good will to men!"

Henry Wandsworth Longfellow

DECEMBER

Glad Christmas comes, and every hearth
    Makes room to give him welcome now,
E'en want will dry its tears in mirth,
    And crown him with a holy bough;
Though tramping 'neath a winter sky,
    O'er snowy paths and rimy stiles,
The housewife sets her spinning by
    To bid him welcome with her smiles.

Each house is swept the day before,
    And windows stuck with evergreens,
The snow is besom'd from the door,
    And comfort crowns the cottage scenes.
Gilt holly, with its thorny pricks,
    And yew and box, with berries small,
These deck the unused candlesticks,
    And pictures hanging by the wall.

Neighbours resume their annual cheer,
    Wishing, with smiles and spirits high,
Glad Christmas and a happy year
    To every morning passer-by;
Milkmaids their Christmas journeys go,
    Accompanied with favour'd swain;
And children pace the crumping snow,
    To taste their granny's cake again.

The shepherd, now no more afraid,
    Since custom doth the chance bestow,
Starts up to kiss the giggling maid
    Beneath the branch of mistletoe
That 'neath each cottage beam is seen,
    With pearl-like berries shining gay;
The shadow still of what hath been,
    Which fashion yearly fades away.

John Clare

43

PASTOR NOODLE'S LIGHT

Jonathan and Thomas were constantly arguing. Whenever they saw each other, which was often because they were next door neighbours, they found something rude to say. One day, Jonathan would criticise Thomas for allowing his cattle to lean over the fence and eat grass from Jonathan's field. The next day Thomas would be angry with Jonathan because nettles from Jonathan's land were spreading on to Thomas's land. Their two wives were close friends, and they longed for Jonathan and Thomas to be friends.

Eventually one winter, the two long suffering women decided that they could stand it no longer. "Christmas will soon be here," they said to their husbands. "It's supposed to be the season of peace and goodwill. Surely you can learn to be at peace with each other and stop arguing."

But the very next day, Thomas accused Jonathan of shovelling snow on to his land – and a fierce argument arose.

So their wives went to Pastor Noodle to see if he could find an answer.

Pastor Noodle thought for a few moments, stroking his long white beard. Finally he spoke. "I think I have an answer. Leave it to me." Pastor Noodle went immediately to see Jonathan and Thomas, calling them together outside their houses.

"I want you to enter a competition with me on Christmas Eve," Pastor Noodle began. "It will provide entertainment for the whole village. The competition is this. We will divide the barn outside the vicarage into three equal parts. Between dawn and dusk, we will see which of us can fill our part the fullest, using anything we like. If either of you win, you can take all the fruit and vegetables that grow in the garden over the next year. If I win, you must promise never to argue again, and instead learn to be friends."

Jonathan and Thomas thought they had nothing to lose, so they agreed to the competition. At dawn on Christmas Eve, the whole village gathered around the barn.

As soon as the sun was visible above the eastern horizon, Jonathan and Thomas began rushing around the village collecting anything they could find to fill their parts of the barn — bales of straw, old buckets, sacks of potatoes, and whatever else they could carry.

But Pastor Noodle was nowhere to be seen.

At lunch time, Jonathan and Thomas were still busy. And Pastor Noodle was still nowhere to be seen. A few hours later, as the sun began to set below the western horizon, Jonathan and Thomas had both filled their parts of the barn almost to the roof. But Pastor Noodle's part was still completely empty.

Finally, as the last rays of sun were fading, Pastor Noodle came out of his house, carrying an unlit candle. He walked into the barn and placed the candle in the middle. He spoke the verse from the opening chapter of John's Gospel: "The light of Christ shines in the darkness, and the darkness cannot overcome it." Then he knelt down and lit the candle.

In the darkness of Christmas Eve, its light filled the whole barn, shining right up into the rafters of the roof. A great cheer arose as everyone realised that Pastor Noodle had won the competition. Jonathan and Thomas stepped forward. Standing over the candle, they shook hands. And from that Christmas onwards, they were the firmest of friends.

QUOTATIONS

It is good to be children sometimes, and never better than at
Christmas, when its mighty Founder was a child Himself.

CHARLES DICKENS

Christmas is the season for kindling the fire of hospitality in the hall,
the genial flame of charity in the heart.

WASHINGTON IRVING

The coming of Christ by way of a Bethlehem manger seems strange
and stunning. But when we take him out of the manger and invite
him into our hearts, then the meaning unfolds and the strangeness
vanishes.

NEIL C. STRAIT

I hope your Christmas has had a little touch of Eternity in among
the rush and pitter and all. It always seems such a mixture of this
world and the next – but that after all is the idea!

EVELYN UNDERHILL *LETTERS*

No trumpet blast profaned
The home in which the Prince of Peace was born.
No bloody streamlet stained
Earth's silver ridges on that sacred morn.

WILLIAM CULLEN BRYANT *CHRISTMAS IN 1875*

Christmas is the day that holds all time together.

ALEXANDER SMITH

The fact of Jesus' coming is the final and unanswerable proof that
God cares.

WILLIAM BARCLAY

THE LITTLE FIR TREE

From a story by Hans Christian Andersen

This is the story of a fir tree. It had been planted in the forest when it was only two feet high. Although at first the forest seemed strange and frightening, the fir tree learned to love the birds and animals that lived there. It made special friends with a robin which often perched on its tiny branches.

Each autumn, the woodcutters used to cut down the biggest fir trees. It was quite terrifying to hear the creaking and thud as the great tree fell. Then the woodcutters dragged the trees out of the forest.

"Why are they cutting down the trees?" the little tree asked the robin. "And where are they taking them?"

"Well," said the robin, "they strip off the branches and the trunks make magnificent masts for sailing ships. Those trees will sail across the sea and visit all the countries of the world."

The little fir tree was thrilled. It dreamt that one day it might be cut down and turned into a proud mast.

Then in December the woodcutters came a second time. But now it was the small trees they cut, the ones only five or six feet tall.

"Why are they cutting down the small trees?"
the fir tree asked.

"Well," replied the robin, "they take the little trees to the markets and families buy them to put in their houses. They decorate them with candles and gold balls and silver tinsel and put a star on top."

The little fir tree dreamed of standing in some grand house But after a few years it had grown to eight feet and was beginning to despair of being a decorated tree. Then one December, two woodcutters came and had a close look at it.

"Yes, just the job," said one.

"It'll be just right for the manor house, they need a tall one," said the other.

So the first man lifted his axe and brought it down on the little tree. Ugh! And as they dragged it away from the forest, it felt helpless and frightened. It was taken for a bumpy ride on the back of a cart to a grand manor house. Three servants collected the tree from the cart. They carried it into the living room and began to decorate it.

At tea time, five noisy children were allowed in. They charged up to the tree so fast that it thought it would be pushed over. But the children swerved in time and began running around it, shouting with excitement. Once it had got over the shock, the tree began to enjoy the noise and bustle. Eventually the children were taken off to bed, and later that night, the mother and father came in and laid their presents at the base of the tree.

The next day, there was even more excitement as the children rushed to open their presents. Later on, the family and the servants sat round the tree singing carols. By the end of the evening. the tree's head was spinning. This had been the most exciting day of its life. And it felt so happy because it was giving these people such pleasure. As it went to sleep, it looked forward happily to the coming days and weeks.

The next day was much quieter. Everyone seemed tired, and there were no more presents. Then – what a shock! Twelve days after Christmas, the servants came and stripped all the decorations off the tree. They picked it up, carried it outside – and threw it into a dark shed.

For three months, the tree lay in the shed, utterly miserable. Why had they turned against it, when it had given them so much happiness? Why had they treated it so roughly? It thought of the robin, the rabbits and the squirrels in the forest, and it longed to be among them. The joy of Christmas now seemed like a dream.

Then one morning, the servants came to the shed and pulled the tree out on to the ground. The servants hacked it up, put it in a basket and carried into the house. And later that day, it was thrown log by log onto the fire.

The pain was terrible. As the tree lay there dying, it could hear a hymn being sung in the church opposite the house.

"When I survey the wondrous cross
On which the Prince of Glory died,
My richest gain I count but loss,
And pour contempt on all my pride."

It was Good Friday.

The next morning, the ash from the grate was cleared and put in a basket in the yard. And the following day, Easter Sunday, the basket was tipped on to the vegetable garden.

That spring, seeds were sown in that soil. And it was ash from our little fir tree that enabled those seeds to grow into fine vegetables.

SILENT NIGHT

1

Silent night! Holy night!
    All is calm, all is bright,
Round yon virgin mother and child;
    Holy infant, so tender and mild,
Sleep in heavenly peace,
    Sleep in heavenly peace.

2

Silent night! Holy night!
    Shepherds quail at the sight;
Glories stream from heaven afar,
    Heavenly hosts sing Alleluia!
Christ the Saviour is born.
    Christ the Saviour is born.

3

Silent night! Holy night!
    Son of God, love's pure light
Radiant beams from thy holy face,
    With the dawn of redeeming grace,
Jesus, Lord, at thy birth,
    Jesus, Lord, at thy birth.

Joseph Mohr (1792-1848)
translated by John Freeman Young (1820-85)

THE THIRD LAMB

From a story by Anne D. Kyle

In the village of Fals in Italy, there lived a woodcarver called Dritte. For many years Dritte had made exquisite carvings for the churches of Austria and Italy. But now no more carvings were needed. Dritte and his wife Beata were afraid they would starve.

Beata said, "Do you think it would be wicked to make carvings that are not for churches?"

"Beata!" Dritte exclaimed. "God taught me to carve only for his glory."

Dritte went sadly to his workshop. A boy was playing there with the animals that knelt round a manger scene. Who was this cheeky child? Not one of the village children. Perhaps a visitor. He was a beautiful boy with hair as softly glowing as the gold upon the altar. The boy picked up the white lamb.

"Boy!" Dritte called. "Those aren't ordinary animals. They worship the baby. You mustn't touch them."

"But the baby doesn't mind," the boy said. "I wish to take this lamb with me. I have no toys to play with when it's cold in the mountains."

"Put the lamb back," Dritte said gently. "And I'll make you another. One that nods its head when you touch it."

"Will you? When will it be ready?"

"Come for it tomorrow," Dritte said. "Where do you live?"

The boy waved his hand vaguely upward. "Out there. My father and I together. Goodbye, sir, and thank you."

Dritte began to carve a lamb. "Since it is a gift, and not for sale, it can't matter that it's not for the church," he said. It was finished for the next day. As he was admiring it, a shadow fell across the doorway. "Come in," he called. At the door was a shivering girl from the group of travelling musicians.

"What do you want, child?"

"Scraps of food, there are none to spare in the village. My father will beat me if I return with my basket empty. Unless, if I took this little lamb, he would not beat me."

"Take it," Dritte said.

The girl hugged the lamb and darted away. As Dritte was finishing his second lamb, some of the village children burst in. When they saw the little lamb with its nodding head, they longed to have it.

Dritte said, "I've promised this lamb to someone else, but I will make each of you a little animal — what would you like?"

"A donkey that will shake its ears."

"A rooster that will flap its wings."

"And you?" said Dritte to little Drino.

"There's no time," said Drino. "The priest is sending me

to the orphanage. Please, may I have this lamb?"

"Here, take it," Dritte said.

Early next morning, Dritte started work on the third lamb. After a few days, the village children took away their animals, but the third lamb stood waiting.

A week later, Beata said, "The whole village is talking about the wonderful animals you have made. They beg you to teach them how to carve. We'll sell the toys and the village will have money again."

"Beata," Dritte cried out. "I can't do this, even if I starve, unless God gives me a sign." Deeply troubled, Dritte rushed outside. In the street he bumped into the priest.

"I'm sorry," he said. "I wasn't looking. I was so full of my troubles."

"Yes," said the priest. "We all have troubles. And the priest told Dritte about little Marte, who had fallen and broken her back. "All day she lies flat," said the priest. "Yesterday a band of travelling musicians stopped at her village, telling fortunes. Her father invited them in to amuse his daughter. But all she wanted was a carved lamb that nodded its head.

"Why!" Dritte said. "That's the lamb I made."

"Well you are the very man I want," said the priest. "Will you carve a lamb for Marte? Her father will pay you well."

"I want no pay," Dritte said. "I have a lamb here. I'll take it this afternoon."

As he set out up the mountainside, Dritte felt the sting of snow on his cheeks. It was a relief to arrive and give Marte her lamb. Then at last he arrived home again, he was cold and weary.

His workshop was dark. He raised his lantern and there in the corner he imagined he saw a boy.

"I gave your lamb away," Dritte said. "I'll make you another."

He heard in his mind a boy saying. "The lambs you gave to the travellers' child, to Drino, and to Marte, you also gave to me."

"But I don't understand," Dritte said.

The voice replied. "Oh Dritte, there are many ways of serving God. You brought joy to three children. ' Whatever you did for one of the least of my brothers, you have done for me '."

THE CHRISTMAS JUGGLER

Barnabas was a juggler. From the age of six he had walked from town to town in central France, juggling in the town squares. At first he went with his father, but when his father died, Barnabas juggled on his own. Juggling was the only thing he knew how to do.

One summer, the weather was so rainy that many of the crops were ruined, and people had very little money to give to Barnabas for his juggling. When autumn came, he trudged along the muddy lanes wondering if he would starve to death.

One day, in late October, Barnabas met a monk on the road.

"Why are you looking so sad?" the monk asked. Barnabas told the monk his story, and at the end, the monk said, "Have you ever thought of becoming a monk? Perhaps God wants you to join our monastery at Clairvaux."

Barnabas was so surprised. He had always said his prayers, but as for being a monk…

"It's hard work, mind you," continued the monk. "We spend six hours a day working in the fields, and another six in church worshipping God."

Barnabas could feel his heart throbbing. He knew that God was speaking to him.

"Yes," he blurted out. "I'll become a monk."

Barnabas was happy working each day in the fields. And he loved the six hours spent in church, listening to the beautiful music and prayers. He wished he had become a monk when he was young.

But then he started feeling sad.

"All the other monks have so much to give to God," he thought. "Some can sing, others can read the Bible aloud, or paint pictures for the church. But I'm useless."

As Christmas approached, he became so sad that he could hardly eat his meals or work in the fields. He desperately wanted to do something special for the baby Jesus. But he could think of nothing.

On Christmas Eve, the abbot, who was in charge of the monastery, asked Barnabas to put the nativity figures in the crypt. The crypt was a large cellar under the church where monks often came to pray alone. At one end was a small altar with two candles. So Barnabas took the wooden figures down the stone steps into the crypt. He lit the candles, and carefully placed the figures on the altar. When he had finished, he stepped back to look at the beautiful scene: Mary, Joseph and the baby, with all the animals looking on. Suddenly, he knew exactly what he must do for the baby Jesus.

That evening, Barnabas crept into the monastery larder, and took out six oranges, six bananas and a plate, hiding them under his white habit. At midnight, when the monks proceeded into the church for the great Christmas service, Barnabas slipped out through a side door, and down the steps into the crypt. He stood in front of the crib scene.

"Dearest Jesus," he said, "I'm doing this especially for you."

Then, for an hour an a half, Barnabas juggled and danced, his heart filled with joy.

Unknown to Barnabas, another monk had followed him and was watching him from behind a pillar. After an hour the monk hurried back to tell the abbot.

When the midnight service was over, the abbot led the monks quietly out of the side door, and down to the crypt. Barnabas was concentrating so hard that he did not hear them gather at the back.

At last, Barnabas finished. As he stopped, panting with exhaustion, the monks broke into a great song: "Glory be to God on high, and on earth peace and goodwill to all people."

Barnabas could hardly believe his ears. He thought the archangel Gabriel had come to visit him.

Then the abbot came out of the darkness into the candlelight and embraced Barnabas.

The following morning – Christmas morning – families from all the villages came to worship with the monks. At the end of the service, some monks placed the nativity figures on the main altar of the church. Then the abbot led Barnabas up to the altar, and, to the congregation's astonishment, Barnabas began to juggle. Oranges and bananas flew through the air so fast and so high that it seemed as though they filled the whole church. Then, even while he was still juggling, he balanced a plate on his nose and started to dance. Many of the people had seen Barnabas juggling in town squares, but never had they seen him perform so well as this.

Barnabas remained happy at Clairvaux for the rest of his life. And every Christmas morning, he juggled in front of the nativity figures on the altar.

UNTO US A BOY IS BORN

1

Unto us a boy is born!
    King of all creation,
Came he to a world forlorn,
    The Lord of every nation.

2

Cradled in a stall was he
    With sleepy cows and asses;
But the very beasts could see
    That he all men surpasses.

3

Herod then with fear was filled;
    'A prince,' he said 'in Jewry!'
All the little boys he killed
    At Bethl'em in his fury.

4

Now may Mary's son, who came
    So long ago to love us,
Lead us all with hearts aflame
    Unto the joys above us.

5

Omega and Alpha he!
    Let the organ thunder
While the choir with peals of glee
    Doth rend the air asunder.

LATIN ANON. (15th century)
translated by PERCY DEARMER (1837–1936)

CHRIST IN THE MANGER

1

Child in the manger,
    Infant of Mary,
Outcast and stranger,
    Lord of all!
Child who inherits
    All our transgressions,
All our demerits
    On him fall.

2

Once the most holy
    Child of salvation
Gentle and lowly
    Lived below;
Now as our glorious
    Mighty Redeemer,
See him victorious
    O'er each foe.

3

Prophets foretold him,
    Infant of wonder,
Angels behold him
    On his throne:
Worthy our Saviour
    Of all our praises;
Happy for ever
    Are his own.

Mary MacDonald (1789–1872)

translated by Lachlan MacBean (1853–1931)